Note to parents, carers and teachers

Read it yourself is a series of modern stories, favourite characters and traditional tales written in a simple way for children who are learning to read. The books can be read independently or as part of a guided reading session.

Each book is carefully structured to include many high-frequency words vital for first reading. The sentences on each page are supported closely by pictures to help with understanding, and to offer lively details to talk about.

The books are graded into four levels that progressively introduce wider vocabulary and longer stories as a reader's ability and confidence grows.

Ideas for use

- Although your child will now be progressing towards silent, independent reading, let her know that your help and encouragement is always available.

- Developing readers can be concentrating so hard on the words that they sometimes don't fully grasp the meaning of what they're reading. Answering the puzzle questions at the end of the book will help with understanding.

For more information and advice on Read it yourself and book banding, visit **www.ladybird.com/readityourself**

Book Band 10

Level 4 is ideal for children who are ready to read longer stories with a wider vocabulary and are eager to start reading independently.

Special features:

Detailed illustrations to capture the imagination

Clear type

Longer sentences

Corporal Pig saw his chance. The bird guarding the nest had gone to sleep! The pigs grabbed all three eggs and made off with them.

King Pig was going to be so pleased!

Full, exciting story

There were one or two things that Stella was going to need.
First, she pulled up a big weed.
Then she grabbed an old shawl.
Without explaining, she set off for the slingshot.

Richer, more varied vocabulary

Educational Consultant: Geraldine Taylor
Book Banding Consultant: Kate Ruttle

A catalogue record for this book is available from the British Library

This edition published by Ladybird Books Ltd 2014
80 Strand, London, WC2R 0RL
A Penguin Company

001

The moral right of the author and illustrator has been asserted.

ISBN:978-072328-907-4

Printed in China

Stella and the Egg Tree

Written by Richard Dungworth
Illustrated by Ilias Arahovitis

In Pig City, all was not well. King Pig was in a bad mood. And when King Pig was in a bad mood, it was very bad news for all the other pigs!

"Where are my eggs?" King Pig asked Corporal Pig. "You must have them for me by now!"

Corporal Pig went red and looked down.

"No?" said the king. "WHY NOT?" he yelled.

"It's those rotten birds, Your Majesty," explained Corporal Pig. "They guard their nest so well, day and night. We just can't get to their eggs!"

King Pig looked furious. "Are you telling me that you can't deal with one or two silly little birds?" he yelled. "Get out of here and don't come back without my eggs!"

Later that day, on the other side of Piggy Island...

Red, Chuck, Bomb and the Blues were playing ball. Stella was looking after the eggs. The sun was out and it was making Stella feel a little sleepy.

15

Corporal Pig saw his chance. The bird guarding the nest had gone to sleep! The pigs grabbed all three eggs and made off with them.

King Pig was going to be so pleased!

Stella was NOT pleased. "The eggs!"
she cried. "They've gone!"
The other birds came over.
"The pigs must have taken them,"
said Red furiously.
"What do we do about it?"
said Chuck.

"Not 'we', Chuck," said Stella. She was just as furious as Red. "It's up to me to put things right. I'll get our eggs back. No rotten pig gets away with playing a trick on me!"

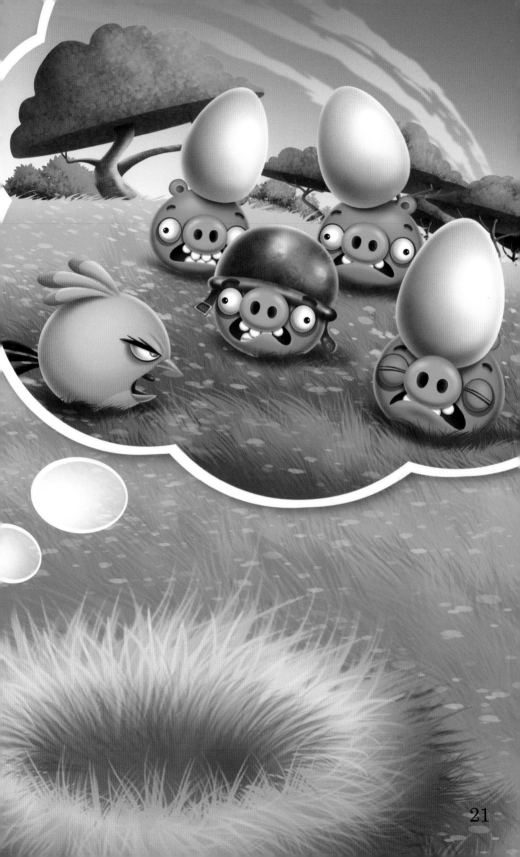

There were one or two things that
Stella was going to need.
First, she pulled up a big weed.
Then she grabbed an old shawl.
Without explaining, she set off for
the slingshot.

The pigs were well on their
way back to Pig City when
they met a stranger. She was
an odd-looking old pig in a shawl.

"Well, my pigs!" she cried.
"Where are you going?"

Corporal Pig was only too
pleased to tell the stranger
his good news.

"We're going back to Pig City,
to see King Pig," he said.
"We have eggs for him –
three big eggs!"

"I'm sure King Pig will be pleased to have them!" said the old pig. "But only three? Is that all? It seems odd to take only three eggs, when King Pig could have as many as he likes!"

Corporal Pig looked at the stranger. "As many as...? But how...?" he said.

The old pig laughed. "I will tell you – for a price!" she said. "But we have no way to pay you," said Corporal Pig.

"You can pay me with an egg,"
said the stranger. "For just one egg,
I will tell you how to get as many
more as you like."

The pigs thought this seemed
like a very good deal.

"You must go to the Evergreen Egg Tree," said the old pig. "There, you will be sure to find all the eggs you need!"

"The Evergreen Egg Tree! Wow!" said Corporal Pig. "But where is it?"

"For that, you must pay another egg!" said the old pig.

"That seems fair," thought Corporal Pig, and he did so.

"The tree grows right in the very middle of an icky swamp," said the stranger.

"That's no good!" cried Corporal Pig. "We can't get to it there!"

The old pig laughed again. "There is another way," she said. "You could grow an Evergreen Egg Tree of your own."

The old pig took something from her shawl. "This shoot comes from the Evergreen Egg Tree," she explained. "It will grow into another tree. You may have it – for just one more egg."

"Silly old things!" laughed Stella, as the pigs went on their way with the weed.

She set off for home to find the other birds and tell them all about her little trick – and to put all three eggs back in their nest.

And as for King Pig? Well, he was not as pleased with the Evergreen Egg Tree as Corporal Pig thought he would be...

How much do you remember about the story
of Angry Birds: Stella and the Egg Tree?
Answer these questions and find out!

- Who is in a bad mood at
  the beginning?

- How many eggs are stolen
  from the birds' nest?

- What does Stella disguise
  herself with?

- Where does Stella tell the pigs they
  will be able to find lots of eggs?

- What does she tell the pigs
  the weed is?

- How many eggs does Corporal Pig
  have for King Pig at the end?

Unjumble these words to make characters from the story, then match them to the correct pictures.

Kgni Pgi   Slalet   Chkuc

Rde   Crolarop Pgi

Read it yourself with Ladybird

Tick the books you've read!

For more confident readers who can read simple stories with help.

Level 3

- YOU won't like this present as much as I DO!
- The Elves and the Shoemaker
- Hansel and Gretel
- Harry and the Bucketful of Dinosaurs
- Jack and the Beanstalk
- The Red Knight

- Furi on Music Island
- Poppet Stows Away
- Rapunzel
- Aladdin
- The Jungle Book
- Roxy and the Great Escape
- Angry Birds Chuck
- Angry Birds Bomb's Best Birthday

Longer stories for more independent, fluent readers.

Level 4

- I am Inventing an Invention
- Harry and the Dinosaurs United
- Heidi
- Katsuma and the Art Thief
- Luvli and the Glump-a-tron
- The Pied Piper of Hamelin

- Sam and the Robots
- Snow White and the Seven Dwarfs
- The Wizard of Oz
- The Little Mermaid
- Alice in Wonderland
- Oddie The Hero
- Angry Birds Red
- Angry Birds Stella